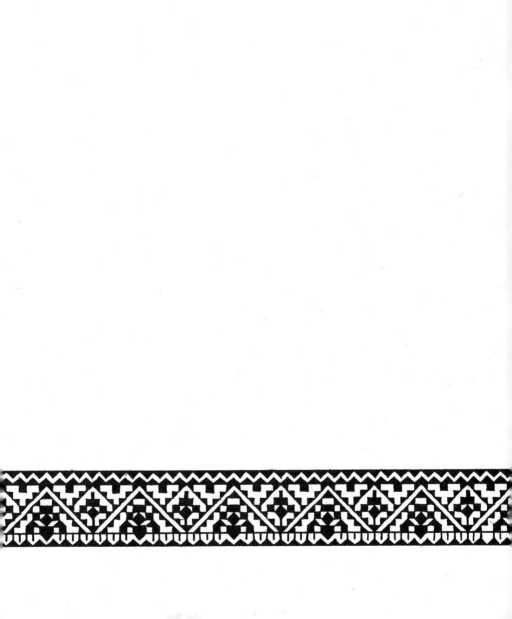

The Twelve
Clever Brothers
and Other Fools

The Twelve Clever Brothers and Other Fools

Folktales from Russia
Collected and Adapted by
MIRRA GINSBURG
Illustrated by
Charles Mikolaycak

J. B. Lippincott · New York

Library of Congress Cataloging in Publication Data

Ginsburg, Mirra.
    The twelve clever brothers and other fools.
    SUMMARY: Fourteen traditional folktales from the
different peoples of Russia featuring both clever
and silly fools.
    1. Tales, Russian. [1. Folklore—Russia]
I. Mikolaycak, Charles. II. Title.
PZ8.1.G455Ts   398.2′1′0947   79-2409
ISBN 0-397-31822-7
ISBN 0-397-31862-6 lib. bdg.

10 9 8 7 6 5 4 3 2 1

First Edition

TO CHUCK   M.G.

TO MIRRA   C.M.

Long Life to Fools!

Contents

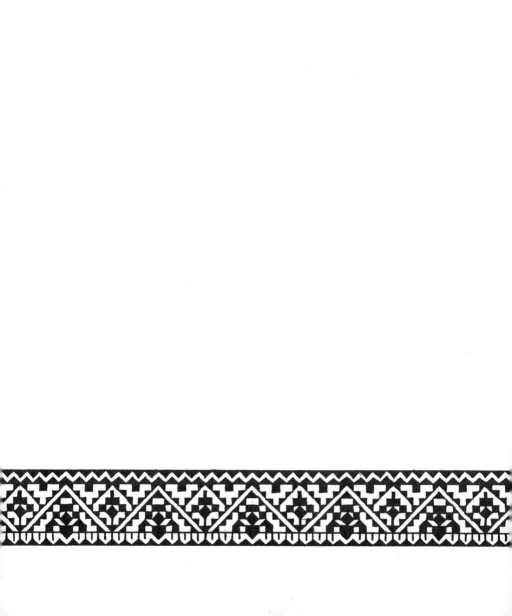

The Twelve
Clever Brothers
and Other Fools

The Twelve Clever Brothers Go to Town

A Veps Tale

At the very end of a village in the far north there were twelve houses, each one exactly like the rest. Six of them were on one side of the street, and six on the other side. The twelve houses belonged to twelve brothers. Each had a wife and children, but this story is not about them, and so we shall not speak of them again.

Well, then, there were twelve brothers. One winter day they harnessed their horses to their sleds and went to town to buy the things they needed. One needed salt, another cotton for his wife's dress, a third soap, a fourth boots.

The journey was a long one, and they were still far from town when night fell. They stopped at an inn and unharnessed their horses. Then one brother said:

"Let us turn our sleds in the direction of town, or we won't know which way to go in the morning."

"Right," said the others. "We have a clever brother."

The innkeeper heard them and laughed, but said nothing.

The brothers took the horses to the stable, and all twelve turned their sleds one way—in the direction of town. After that they came into the inn, had their supper, and went to bed.

When they were asleep, the innkeeper turned the sleds around. "Let me see what those sillies will do."

In the morning the brothers started harnessing their horses, greatly pleased with themselves.

"That was clever of us," said one. "If we

had not turned the sleds last night, we wouldn't know which way to go now."

"The worst thing is to lose your way along an unfamiliar road," said another.

"One head is fine," said a third. "But with twelve, you'll never go astray."

The brothers set out. The innkeeper looked after them, shook his head, but said nothing.

They drove along, whipping their horses, in a hurry to get to town. Suddenly the first in line said:

"Look, brothers, this place somehow looks familiar. It's just like the one we passed yesterday. There's the birch by the boulder, and the ditch by the roadside."

"It does look familiar," said the second.

"There are many places in the world that look alike," said the third.

"Sure," said the fourth. "Hereabouts, every other tree is a birch, and there are boulders and ditches everywhere."

And the twelfth one said:

"Stop gaping, we must hurry."

They drove an hour. Another hour. A third. And no one spoke except to speed his horse.

Then the fifth brother said:

"I have a feeling we passed this village yesterday."

All the brothers turned their heads and looked.

"Not this village," said the sixth.

"No, not this one," said the seventh.

"That village was on the left," said the sixth.

"And this one's on the right," said the seventh.

"Stop arguing," said the twelfth. "We've got to move, or we'll be stuck for the night again."

Again they drove in silence. Another village appeared in the distance. The eighth brother said:

"If I didn't know we're going to town, I'd swear this is our village."

"And there's the hillock, just like ours," said the ninth.

"And there are six houses, just like ours, and six across the street," said the tenth.

"I said there are many places in the world that look alike, didn't I?" the third reminded them.

"You did say that," agreed the eleventh. "But a place like ours, a village like ours, houses like ours—no, you will not find the like of them anywhere in the world."

The twelfth cried angrily:

"Stop babbling! Our village, not ours—we've got to go forward."

He had not finished shouting when a yellow dog ran up to his sled and wagged its tail.

The twelfth one said:

"I don't know whose village this is, but the dog is mine."

"Well, if it's your dog, then it's our village," said the first, and he turned into his yard.

"What's the good of traveling?" said the twelfth. "It's best to stay at home."

And all the brothers nodded in agreement and drove off, each into his own yard.

How Grandpa Mowed the Lord's Meadow

A Chuvash Tale

A rich lord hired grandpa to mow his hay for twenty-five rubles, and drove him in his horse cart to the distant meadow. There he left him with food enough to last him while he worked.

After the lord had gone, grandpa cooked himself some lunch, ate it, and lay down for a nap. In the evening, as the sun was setting, he woke, had his supper, and went to sleep again. In the morning, as the sun was rising, he woke, cooked his breakfast, ate it, and lay down again.

This went on for seven days. When he had no more food left, grandpa returned to the lord and demanded his wages. But the lord was stingy. He did not want to part with twenty-five rubles and gave grandpa only twenty. Grandpa tried to argue with him, but soon he realized he could not win. Then, with a threatening look, he asked the lord:

"So you won't pay me the rest of my wages?"

"I won't," said the lord.

"Is that final?"

"It is final."

"In that case, let all the grass rise back in its place in the meadow," said grandpa, spat, and walked away.

The lord was happy that he had saved five rubles. He harnessed his horse and drove off to look at his hay. But when he came to the meadow, he found all the grass in its place, even taller and greener than before.

"Oh, what a fool I was!" he cried. "I should have given old grandpa his five rubles. Now I will have to pay again to have it mowed a second time!"

And sly old grandpa went home, grinning, with twenty rubles in his pocket.

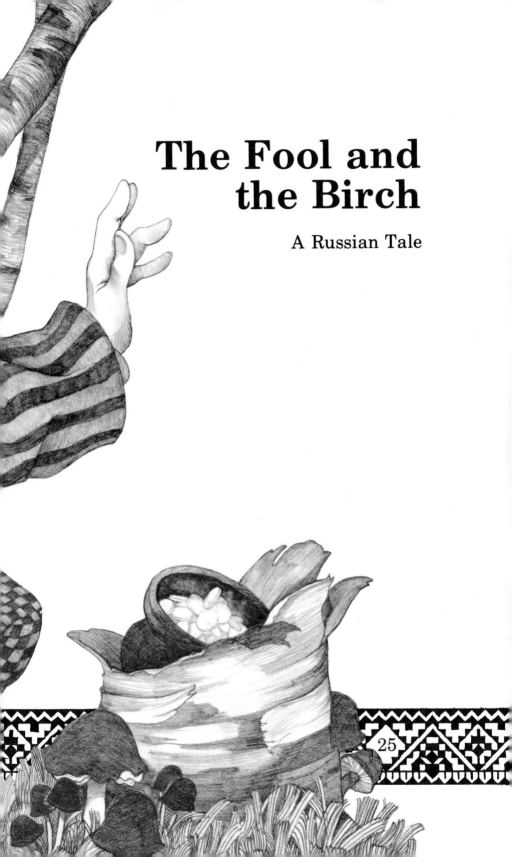

The Fool and the Birch

A Russian Tale

In a faraway land there lived an old man and his three sons. Two were clever, but the youngest was a fool. The old man died, and the sons divided their inheritance by drawing lots. But somehow the elder brothers got the house, the land, and all the goods and money. All that the fool got was an ox, skinny and feeble with age.

On market day the clever brothers loaded their wagons with goods to sell. The fool said, "I'll take my ox to market, too. Somebody may buy it."

The brothers laughed at him. But he tied a rope around the horns of the ox and set out on the road to town. In the woods he came upon an old, dry birch. The wind blew, and the birch creaked—"Cree-cro, cree-cro."

Why is it creaking? thought the fool.

Perhaps it wants to buy my ox.

He stopped and said to the birch:

"Why don't you talk plainly, so I can understand? You want the ox? I'll sell it. Twenty rubles. No, not a kopek less. Fine. Let me have the money."

The birch said nothing but "Cree-cro, cree-cro." And the fool decided it was trying to say, "Tomorrow, tomorrow."

"All right," he agreed. "I'll come for it tomorrow."

He tied the ox to the birch, said goodbye, and went home.

The clever brothers came back from market and asked the fool:

"Well, fool, did you sell your ox?"

"I did."

"How much did you get for it?"

"Twenty rubles."

"Not bad. And where's the money?"

"I didn't get it yet. I have to come for it tomorrow."

"Eh, what a simpleton!"

The next morning the fool got up at dawn, dressed, and went off to collect his money. He came to the woods. The birch stood in the same place, swaying in the wind. The rope hung down from a branch, but the ox wasn't there. It had been eaten by wolves during the night.

"Well, friend," said the fool. "Where is my money? You promised to pay today."

The birch creaked "Cree-cro," and the fool said:

"How can I trust you? Yesterday you said 'tomorrow,' and now it's again 'tomorrow.' Oh, well, I'll wait another day, but not a minute longer. I need the money myself."

He came home, and the clever brothers mocked at him.

"Where is the money?"

"I didn't get it yet. I have to wait another day."

"Who is your buyer?"

"A dry birch in the woods."

"What a fool!"

On the third day the fool took along an axe and went to the woods.

"I want my money."

But the birch only creaked and creaked.

"Oh, no, my friend! If you keep telling me 'tomorrow' and 'tomorrow,' I'll never get paid. You can't play jokes with me. I'll show you!"

Bang! went the axe, and splinters flew in all directions. Now, the dry birch was hollow. And robbers had tucked away a kettle of gold inside it. The birch split in two, and the gold flashed in the sun.

"That's better," said the fool.

He filled his hat and pockets and hurried home.

"Where did you get it?" cried the brothers when he showed them the gold.

"The buyer paid me for the ox," he answered. "And this is only half of it—I couldn't carry more. Let's go and get the rest."

The three of them ran to the woods, and scooped out all the gold, and took it home. They built themselves three houses and lived like lords. And the clever brothers never laughed at the fool again.

This is the end of the tale, and now you may bring me a pitcher of ale.

Eight Donkeys

An Armenian Tale

A merchant decided to sell some of his donkeys. He took seven donkeys, mounted one of them, and went off to market. On the way, he counted the donkeys, and found he had only six. He got off his donkey and counted again. This time he had seven. He mounted again and went on. After a while, he checked once more to see if he had all his donkeys. And again he had only six. He got down, and counted seven. This went on several times. The merchant got more and more worried and decided to walk, to make sure that he wouldn't lose the seventh donkey.

A man came up and asked why he was walking when he could ride, and the merchant explained:

"The moment I mount, I lose a donkey. When I get down, I find him again. Would

you do me a favor, good man? Count the donkeys and tell me how many there are."

The man counted and laughed.

"According to my count, there are
eight."

How Two Brothers Improved Their Luck

A Chuvash Tale

There were two brothers. They were neither rich nor poor, but their larder was empty, their clothes were in rags, and the wind whistled through the cracks in the walls of their hut. Besides, they had no seed to sow their field.

"We're getting richer and richer," said the younger brother one day. "I feel it in my bones."

"Your bones are liars," said the older one. "We'll be lucky if we make ends meet."

They talked things over and decided to go out into the world and try to improve their lot.

The younger brother went ahead and met a fat lord with his fat wife, driving out in a three-horse carriage to admire the peas in their field. And their crop was a good one indeed.

"We have fine peas this year," said the lord.

"You call that peas?" said the younger brother. "Now, our lord has a crop—three horses can barely carry a single pea!"

"You're fooling, my friend. There are no such peas in the world."

"Well, if I'm a liar, ask Truth. He's right behind me," said the young man, and went on.

Soon the older brother came down the road. The lord stopped him and asked:

"A liar passed here just before. He said his lord grew peas so big that three horses could barely carry a single pea. Is that true?"

"I haven't seen the peas," answered the older brother. "But I've seen an empty pea pod. Eight men rowed across the river in it."

"Can you get us some seed of those peas?"

"I can. But it will cost you a hundred rubles."

The lord gave the man a hundred rubles, and he went on.

Meantime, the younger brother came to another lord's field. This lord, who was even fatter than the first, had also driven out with his wife, to admire his cabbages.

"We've got a splendid crop of cabbages this year," said the lord to his wife.

"You call that cabbages?" the young man said. "Now, our lord has grown cabbages—you need six horses to cart a single one away from the field."

"You're fooling. There are no such cabbages in the world."

"Well, if I'm a liar, ask Truth. He's right behind me," said the young man, and went on.

Soon the older brother came down the road. The lord stopped him and asked:

"A liar passed here just before. He said his lord grows cabbages so big that it takes six horses to cart each one from the field. Is that true?"

"I haven't seen the cabbages," answered the older brother. "But I've seen a regiment of soldiers resting in the shade of a single leaf."

"Can you get me the seeds of that cabbage?"

"I can. But it will cost you a hundred rubles."

The lord gave the man a hundred rubles, and he went on.

By this time, the younger brother had reached the city, and he stopped to look at a tall new house. Its owner and his wife, all

dressed in silk and velvet, stood in the street, admiring their house.

"It is a palace, not a house! No one in the country has the like of it."

"You call that a palace?" said the young man. "Now, my master built himself a palace—if you look up, your hat will tumble off your head, and still you will not see the top."

"You're fooling. There is no house in the land that's taller than ours."

"Well, if I'm a liar, ask Truth. He's right behind me," said the young man, and went on.

Soon the older brother came up the street. The owner of the new house stopped him and asked:

"A liar passed here just before. He said his master has a house so high that, if you look up, your hat will tumble off your head, and still you will not see the top. Is that true?"

"I haven't seen any hats tumbling," the man answered. "But I did hear of a rooster flying to the top and pecking up half the moon."

"Can you find me the builder of that house?"

"I can. But he's a long way off, and I will need two hundred rubles for the journey."

The owner of the new house gave the man two hundred rubles, and he hurried on, to catch up with his younger brother.

They went home, patched up their hut, sowed their field, got themselves good wives, and lived in peace and plenty ever after.

The Crooked Pine

A Tatar Tale

Many years ago there lived a rich man who was very pleased with himself.

"No one can fool me!" he would boast. "I am the cleverest man in the land."

"You are," his wife would flatter him. "But look out for Mahmoud."

"You are, you are," his friends would flatter him. "But look out for Mahmoud. He's poor, but he is clever."

One day the rich man rode through the woods and saw Mahmoud leaning against a crooked pine.

"Well met, Mahmoud," he said. "I hear you are a famous trickster. But no one has ever fooled me. Let's see if you can."

"I'd be glad to try," said Mahmoud. "Unfortunately, I left my bag of tricks at home."

"Go bring it here. I'll wait."

"My home is far away—it will take too long."

"Then get up on my horse behind me. We'll ride over."

"And what about the pine? You see how crooked it is? If I don't hold it up, it will topple."

"Very well, I'll stay and hold it up for you till you return. But hurry."

Mahmoud got on the horse and rode off at a gallop.

And the rich man, they say, is still there, holding up the pine.

The Clever Fool

A Latvian Tale

A father had three sons. Two were clever, the third was a fool. The father built a new house and said that he would give the house to the son who would fill it all up.

The oldest son brought a horse into the house. But the horse took up only one corner.

The middle son pulled a wagon full of hay into the house. But the hay took up only half the house.

Then came the fool's turn. He brought in a big candle and lit it. The whole house was filled with light.

And so it was the fool who got the house.

Tyndal
and the Priest

A Moldavian Tale

53

There lived a man called Tyndal.

Once Tyndal went to visit his cousins in a distant village. He walked and walked, till evening fell, and he decided to spend the night at an inn.

He knocked. A woman opened the door and said:

"Come in, come in. I have another traveler here, a priest. You can share a room and keep each other company."

"Wake me early," said Tyndal before going to bed.

"Don't wake me," said the priest. "I'll get up when I've slept enough."

The woman roused Tyndal before dawn. He dressed quickly in the dark and hurried out.

When the sun came up, he glanced down

at himself and saw the priest's robe instead of his own coat. He stopped in anger. "Now I'll have to go all the way back," he cried. "That fool of a woman woke the priest instead of me."

Tyndal
Goes to Market

A Moldavian Tale

Tyndal's wife sent him to market to buy milk and eggs. Off he went, but he didn't take a pitcher and a basket with him.

He came to market and started thinking, How will I get my purchases home? "Well," he said to himself, "that's easy." He took off his hat and told the storekeeper to pour the milk in.

"Now," he said, "what about the eggs?"

He thought and thought, and found a solution.

"I'll turn the hat inside out, and it will be just right for the eggs."

No sooner said than done. He got the eggs and marched off home, never noticing what happened to the milk.

"You brought the eggs," his wife said when he came. "And where's the milk?"

"Why, here!" he said, and started turning the hat right side out.

Plop! went the eggs, the way of the milk. And that was how clever Tyndal shopped for milk and eggs.

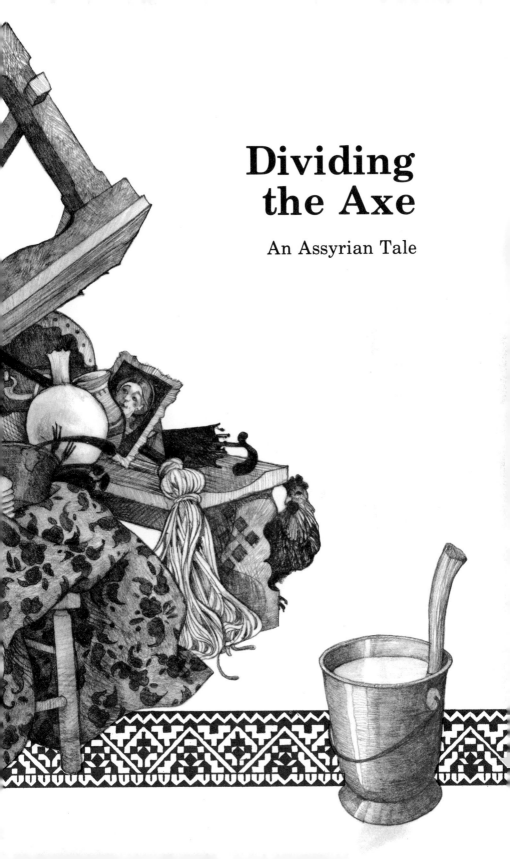

Dividing
the Axe

An Assyrian Tale

Two brothers lived together in peace and harmony. But their wives quarreled all the time, and after a while the brothers started quarreling, too.

"This won't do," they said, and decided to divide their belongings, share and share alike, and set up separate households.

They divided their cattle, their sheep, their geese, and their chickens. They divided their chairs, and their benches, and their pillows, and their pots and pans. They even cut the long dining table in two, so that each got exactly one half.

Then they came to the last thing they owned together—an axe—and they could not decide how to divide it. The wooden handle could be sawed in half. But what about the iron head? They thought, and they talked, and they argued and almost came to blows.

Finally, the older brother said:

"I've found a way. Let's put the axe into a pail of water till it softens. And meantime, we shall hold our tongues and cool our tempers."

And that was what they did. The axe is still soaking in the pail. The brothers are still waiting for it to soften. And they still don't talk to each other.

The Vain
Lord

A Latvian Tale

There was a rich lord who was very vain. He wanted to be noticed by everyone. But he was not very bright, and he was not remarkable in any way, and no one paid him any attention. So he decided that he would become the best-dressed man in town, and then he'd surely be noticed and admired.

He ordered himself a fine suit of clothes, and when the tailor finished it he put it on and went into the marketplace. He walked this way and that, he did all he could to impress everyone he met, but people were busy buying and selling, and no one looked at him.

The lord went back to the tailor and told him to make another suit, of the best and most expensive cloth he could find. When it was ready, the lord put it on and went into the marketplace again. He marched and he strutted in his elegant new clothes, but again no one paid any attention.

The lord raged and ranted. He scolded the tailor and threatened to drive the poor man out of town if he did not make him a suit of clothes that was sure to draw every eye to him.

The frightened tailor did not sleep all night. By morning he had found an answer. He bought the hide of a spotted cow and some burlap sacks like those in which the peasants kept onions and potatoes. He patched them all together and made a new suit for the lord.

The lord put on his suit and went to market. And lo and behold! Not a man or a woman failed to stare at him. And crowds of people followed him wherever he went.

And the vain lord walked with his head high. At long, long last his cherished dream had come true.

The Wolf Cub

An Assyrian Tale

A peasant found a wolf cub in the woods. He took him home and started feeding him goat's milk. "If the wolf cub grows up with my goats," he said to himself, "he'll watch my flock and keep the other wolves away." The cub grew big and strong, and one day he attacked a goat and killed it. Strange, his master wondered. Who could have told him that his father was a wolf?

Barter

A Russian Tale

A poor old peasant swept his barn and found a grain of wheat. He took it to his wife in the kitchen and said to her:

"Get to work, wife. Roast this grain in the oven, grind it into flour, and make a nice bowl of pudding. I shall take the pudding to the king, and he may give me a rich reward."

The peasant's wife made the pudding, and he brought it to the king in the palace.

"M-mm, good!" said the king, licking his lips, and he gave the peasant a golden hen.

The peasant took the hen under his arm and set out homeward. In a field he came upon a herd of horses and a herdsman sitting quietly nearby.

"Where have you been, my good man?" asked the herdsman.

"In the palace. I brought the king a bowl of pudding."

"What did he give you for it?"

"A golden hen."

"Will you barter the hen for a horse?"

The peasant gave the herdsman the golden hen, mounted the horse, and rode off.

He came to another field, where a cowherd was grazing a herd of cows.

"Where have you been, my good man?" asked the cowherd.

"In the palace. I brought the king a bowl of pudding."

"What did he give you for it?"

"A golden hen."

"Where is the golden hen?"

"I bartered it for a horse."

"Will you barter the horse for a cow?"

The peasant gave the cowherd his horse, and led off the cow by the horns. Then he came upon a flock of sheep on a hillside.

"Where have you been, my good man?" asked the shepherd.

"In the palace. I brought the king a bowl of pudding."

"What did he give you for it?"

"A golden hen."

"Where is the golden hen?"

"I bartered it for a horse."

"Where is the horse?"

"I bartered it for a cow."

"Will you barter the cow for a sheep?"

The peasant gave the shepherd his cow and went off with the sheep. Then he came upon a swineherd.

"Where have you been, my good man?" asked the swineherd.

"In the palace. I brought the king a bowl of pudding."

"What did he give you for it?"

"A golden hen."

"Where is the golden hen?"

"I bartered it for a horse."

"Where is the horse?"

"I bartered it for a cow."

"Where is the cow?"

"I bartered it for a sheep."

"Will you barter the sheep for a hog?"

The peasant gave the swineherd his sheep and went on with the hog. By and by he came upon a flock of geese.

"Where have you been, uncle?" asked the goosegirl.

"In the palace. I brought the king a bowl of pudding."

"What did he give you for it?"

"A golden hen."

"Where is the golden hen?"

"I bartered it for a horse."

"Where is the horse?"

"I bartered it for a cow."

"Where is the cow?"

"I bartered it for a sheep."

"Where is the sheep?"

"I bartered it for a hog."

"Will you barter the hog for a goose?"

The peasant gave the girl his hog and went on, driving the goose before him with a willow twig. Then he came upon some boys playing stickball.

"Where have you been, neighbor?" the boys asked him.

"In the palace. I brought the king a bowl of pudding."

"What did the king give you for it?"

"A golden hen."

"Where is the golden hen?"

"I bartered it for a horse."

"Where is the horse?"

"I bartered it for a cow."

"Where is the cow?"

"I bartered it for a sheep."

"Where is the sheep?"

"I bartered it for a hog."

"Where is the hog?"

"I bartered it for a goose."

"Will you barter the goose for a stick?"

The peasant gave the boys his goose and walked on, leaning on the stick. When he came to his house, he put the stick against the fence and went in.

"Well, what did the king give you?" asked his wife.

"He gave me a golden hen."

"Where is the golden hen?"

"I bartered it for a horse."

"Where is the horse?"

"I bartered it for a cow."

"Where is the cow?"

"I bartered it for a sheep."

"Where is the sheep?"

"I bartered it for a hog."

"Where is the hog?"

"I bartered it for a goose."

"Where is the goose?"

"I bartered it for a stick."

"Where is the stick?"

"Outside, by the gate."

The peasant's wife went out into the yard, and took the stick, and started thrashing her husband. And every time she brought the stick down on his back, she cried:

"This is for the golden hen!
And this is for the horse!
And this is for the cow!
And this is for the sheep!
And this is for the hog!
And this is for the goose!
And this is for the stick!
And this is for you!
Don't barter again, you old fool!
Don't barter again!"

How the Twelve Clever Brothers Got Their Feet Mixed Up

A Veps Tale

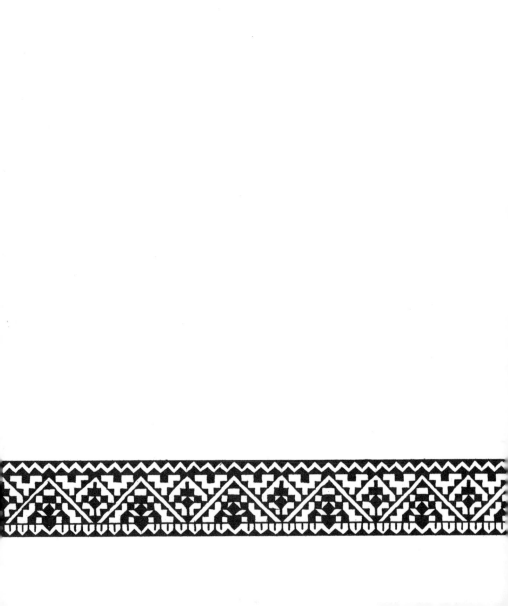

One summer day the twelve clever brothers went to mow their fields. All day long they swung their scythes. By evening, there was a lot of hay, and still a lot of grass. They decided to spend the night in the field so they would lose no time and could start work with the sun.

"How shall we lie down?" asked one of the brothers.

"Side by side, from the youngest to the eldest," said another.

They lay down side by side. Suddenly the eldest said:

"It isn't right. Everybody's in the middle—only I am at the end. I'll get cold at night, and I'm the eldest, too."

"I'm also at the end," said the youngest. "I'll be cold, too, and I'm the youngest."

"Right you are," said the sixth. "It isn't right."

"It isn't," said the seventh. "Why don't you two lie down between us? Then you'll be in the middle."

The first and the twelfth lay down between the sixth and the seventh. But then the second and the eleventh shouted:

"Now we're at the end—we'll be cold!"

Again they changed places, then again, and again, till the first and the twelfth were once more at the ends.

"How did this happen?" they wondered. "Guess we'll have to start all over again."

At that moment, their neighbor happened to be driving by, coming home from mowing his field. He heard the brothers shouting and arguing, and stopped to see what it was all about. The brothers saw him and cried:

"Good evening, and welcome to you! Perhaps you can advise us what to do."

"What's wrong?" he asked.

"Well," they said, "we don't know how to lie down for the night. No matter what we do, there are always two at the ends."

"That's simple," said the neighbor. He stuck a willow twig in the ground and said:

"Lie down with your feet to the twig, and your heads away from the twig."

He said it and drove away.

The brothers lay down as he had told them. Fine! The first now had the twelfth and the second on either side of him, the twelfth had the first and the eleventh. . . . No one was at the end, everyone was in the middle.

At dawn the neighbor drove by again on the way to his field. And again he found the brothers shouting and arguing. Another minute, and they'd come to blows.

"That's my foot!" yelled the seventh.

"What do you mean, yours?" argued the twelfth. "It's mine!"

"Take a look! That cracked toenail is on my foot, not yours," cried the seventh.

"If the toenail is cracked, it's my foot," shouted the first. "I split it with an axe three years ago when I was chopping wood. I want my foot back, and that's all there is to it!"

"What's going on here?" asked the neighbor.

"We can't make head or tail of our feet," the brothers explained. "Our heads are apart, but our feet are mixed up. It's time to mow, and we can't get up."

"That's easy, too," said the neighbor. "Just wait a second, I'll help you."

He pulled out the twig and—whish!—it came down on the brothers' soles. "Ouch!" In a moment, all the brothers were up, each on his own feet. It didn't take them long this time to find which feet belonged to whom.

"Thank you kindly, neighbor," they cried. They jumped up and down on the grass for a while to cool their soles in the morning dew, then went to work.

From that day on, the brothers never stayed in the field at night, afraid they might get their feet mixed up again. "Who knows?" they said. "The neighbor might come by, or he might take another road. And what would we do then?"

MIRRA GINSBURG spent her childhood in a small town in Byelorussia and has been involved with Russian folklore ever since. As an editor, translator, adaptor, and storyteller, she is responsible for more than forty books, over half of them for young readers. Ms. Ginsburg lives in New York City.

CHARLES MIKOLAYCAK received his BFA degree from Pratt Institute. After a number of years as a book designer, he now devotes full time to illustration, with over twenty-five children's books to his credit. He lives in New York City.

Ms. Ginsburg and Mr. Mikolaycak previously collaborated on *How Wilka Went to Sea*, an ALA Notable Book.

THE TWELVE CLEVER BROTHERS AND OTHER FOOLS

Designed by Charles Mikolaycak
Composed by Book Composition Services in 14/18
Century Schoolbook with display in Century Bold
Printed by The Book Press
Bound by The Book Press
Illustrations executed in pencil